Elle
the Thumbelina
Fairy

Special thanks to
Rachel Elliot

ORCHARD BOOKS

First published in Great Britain in 2016 by The Watts Publishing Group

3 5 7 9 10 8 6 4 2

© 2016 Rainbow Magic Limited.
© 2016 HIT Entertainment Limited.
Illustrations © Orchard Books 2016

HIT entertainment

A CIP catalogue record for this book is available from the British Library.

ISBN 978 1 40834 894 9

Printed in Great Britain

MIX
Paper from
responsible sources
FSC® C104740

FSC
www.fsc.org

The paper and board used in this book are made from wood from responsible sources

Orchard Books
An imprint of Hachette Children's Group
Part of The Watts Publishing Group Limited
Carmelite House, 50 Victoria Embankment, London EC4Y 0DZ

An Hachette UK Company
www.hachette.co.uk
www.hachettechildrens.co.uk

Elle
the Thumbelina
Fairy

by Daisy Meadows

ORCHARD

www.rainbowmagic.co.uk

The Fairyland Palace

Fairyland Library

The Three Bears' Cottage

Island

Thumbelina's Cottage

Storybook World

Rapunzel's Tower

Red Riding Hood's Grandmother's House

Red Riding Hood Woods

Jack Frost's Spell

The fairies want stories to stay just the same.
But I've planned a funny and mischievous game.
I'll change all their tales without further ado,
By adding some tricks and a goblin or two!

The four magic stories will soon be improved
When everything soppy and sweet is removed.
Their daft happy endings are ruined and lost,
For no one's as clever as handsome Jack Frost!

Contents

The Storytelling Festival

Rachel Walker skipped along the riverside path, enjoying the warmth of the sun and the scent of flowers in the air. Her best friend, Kirsty Tate, did a cartwheel beside her and laughed. It was always exciting to spend a weekend

together, but this weekend was going to
be extra special. They were going to the
Wetherbury Storytelling Festival, and
they could hardly wait.

"Hurry up, Mum!" called Kirsty,
looking back along the path. "It's almost
time!"

Their favourite author, Alana Yarn,
was going to be sharing her best
storytelling tips, and the girls were really
looking forward to seeing her.

"Don't worry, we won't be late,"
said Mrs Tate with a smile. "Look, the
festival tents are just up ahead. Besides,
my cartwheeling days are over, Kirsty."

"I'm never going to stop doing
cartwheels, even when I'm grown up,"
said Kirsty.

She grinned at Rachel.

They reached the bright festival tents, which were decorated with bunting and huge book pages.

"They look as if they come from a giant's book," said Rachel in delight.

"I do miss getting lost in storybook worlds," said Mrs Tate. "The books I loved best as a child were filled with imaginary things like magic and fairies."

Kirsty and Rachel exchanged a smile. They knew that fairies were real, not imaginary! In fact they had lots of fairy friends, but they were the only two people who knew about it.

"Oh look!" Kirsty exclaimed.

She pointed to where a boat was moored by the riverbank. There was a sign on the path beside it, saying 'Story Barge', and the boat itself was piled high with books. A man was standing on the barge, smiling at them.

"Are you here to see Alana Yarn?" he called.

The girls nodded, and Mrs Tate smiled.

"Have fun, both of you," she said. "I'll see you later."

She hugged them goodbye and then they skipped over to the Story Barge.

"Welcome to the Storytelling Festival," the man said. "Alana Yarn is about to start. Go and sit over there, in the grassy hollow. She won't be long!"

Rachel and Kirsty hurried over to where a large group of

13

children was sitting on cushions.
They were in a circle around a bench,
which was shaped like a book. There
weren't very many empty cushions left,
but the girls found two next to each
other and sat down.

"I feel as if I might burst, I'm so
excited!" said Rachel.

"Me too," Kirsty replied. "I can't
believe that Alana Yarn is actually

going to be here!"

They had read all Alana Yarn's books, and had even queued up in bookshops when a new one came out. The other children in the group looked thrilled too.

"She's here!" someone exclaimed.

Heads bobbed and necks craned as everyone tried to see the famous author. Rachel and Kirsty glimpsed a mane of curly black hair. Then Alana Yarn took her seat on the book-bench, and smiled around at her audience. She had a wide, warm smile and sparkling blue eyes with thick, black lashes. "Welcome to the

Wetherbury Storytelling Festival," said Alana. "I hope you're as excited as I am about this weekend. I want you all to be inspired to tell stories yourselves, and to let your imaginations soar. At the end of the weekend, you will all have the chance to tell a story of your own, using the new skills you've learned. Are there any questions?"

Rachel felt as if she was fizzing with questions! She put up her hand, and Alana nodded at her.

"How do you bring a story to life?" she asked.

"Sometimes the simplest way is the

best," Alana replied. "Right now we're going to begin by reading aloud."

There was a stack of books beside her, which she handed into the crowd of children.

"Make sure everyone gets a copy," she said.

When Rachel and Kirsty got their copies, Kirsty gave a little squeak of happiness. The book they were going to read was *Thumbelina* – one of her favourite stories.

A Magical Library

"Follow the story in your own book," said Alana, opening her copy and starting to read aloud. "Once upon a time there was a woman who longed for children, but had none. At last she went to visit a fairy, and said…"

Rachel and Kirsty were swept up in the story. Alana had a lovely reading voice, and the girls felt as if they could almost see tiny Thumbelina in her happy home, sleeping in her little walnut-shell bed.

"One night, when Thumbelina was asleep under her rose-petal quilt, a

goblin crept in through the window,"
Alana read. "The goblin thought that
Thumbelina would make a pretty wife
for him, so he scooped up the walnut-
shell bed and jumped out of the window
into the garden."

Kirsty and Rachel glanced at each
other.

"That isn't how the story is supposed to
go," Kirsty whispered.

"But that's what it says in the book,"
Rachel replied in a low voice. "Look!"

Kirsty frowned and put up her hand.
Alana stopped reading.

"Is everything all right?" she asked in a
kind voice.

"I'm sorry to interrupt," said Kirsty,
"but I think these books have a mistake
in them. Thumbelina is supposed to be

carried away by a toad, not a goblin."

"Oh!" said Alana, looking surprised. "I'm certain that it's a goblin. After all, that's what the book says."

All the other children in the circle shot puzzled glances at Kirsty. They obviously thought that she was wrong too.

"She's right," said Rachel in a loud voice.

But the other children were shaking their heads and making hushing noises. Alana started reading the story again, and Kirsty looked at Rachel with a worried expression.

"Something's wrong," she whispered. "I know this story very well and there definitely aren't any goblins in it!"

Just then, the empty cushion beside

Rachel gave a little quiver. Kirsty and
Rachel stared at it in astonishment.
The other children were gazing at
Alana, so no one else noticed as the
cushion hopped, shook and jumped.
Then, surrounded by a sprinkle of
pale-blue fairy dust,
a beautiful fairy
fluttered out
from under the
cushion.

"Hello!"
she said in an
excited whisper.
"I'm Elle the
Thumbelina
Fairy, and I've
come to take you
both to Fairyland!"

Rachel and Kirsty were so surprised that they stared at Elle in silence for a moment. She was as tiny as Thumbelina herself, with long wavy hair and an exquisite pale-blue dress. Her wings were dusky pink with curly tips, and her shoes were a delicate shade of lilac.

"Will you come?" Elle asked. "We need your help!"

"Of course we will," said Rachel.

"But how can we leave now? We're
surrounded by other children."

Elle smiled.

"Stories make their own magic,"
she whispered. "The others are too
spellbound by the story to notice what's
happening."

She waved her wand, and there was
a flurry of pale-blue confetti and
glittering thimbles. The girls closed
their eyes as the magic whirled around
them, and when they looked again, they
were standing in a vast library. They
had been transformed into fairies, and
their gossamer wings were fluttering on
their backs.

"Welcome to the Fairyland Library,"
said Elle, giving a delighted twirl.

"It's incredible," Rachel whispered.

"It's the kind of place I've dreamed about," said Kirsty.

The high shelves were a treasure trove of beautiful books with spines in every colour of the rainbow. The arched ceiling was made of glass, flooding the room with natural light. Three deep, squashy chairs with plump cushions were

arranged in a horseshoe shape, and three other fairies were curled up inside them.

"I'd like to introduce you to the other Storybook Fairies," said Elle, leading Rachel and Kirsty forward. "This is Mariana the Goldilocks Fairy, Rosalie the Rapunzel Fairy and Ruth the Red Riding Hood Fairy."

Into the Pages

The other fairies jumped up and smiled at Rachel and Kirsty.

"It's wonderful to meet you," Rachel said, recovering from the surprise of being whisked to Fairyland. "But why have you brought us here?"

"I'm afraid that Jack Frost and his goblins have done something truly terrible," said Elle, sinking into one of the chairs.

She raised her wand and pointed it at one of the bookshelves. A large book swept itself off the shelf, opened in midair and showed a big, blank page. As it hovered there, blurry pictures began to appear on

the page. The pictures grew clearer and the girls drew in their breaths.

"It's a picture of this library," said Kirsty.

"With Jack Frost and his goblins sneaking around inside," Rachel added. "What did they do?"

"They took our most precious belongings," said Elle.

The girls watched the picture in the book. Jack Frost undid the golden clasp of a wooden box. He raised the lid and scooped the contents into a bag, laughing. Then he handed the bag to a goblin, threw the box on the floor and left the library.

The picture faded and the book closed itself and slotted back into its place on the shelf.

"What was in the box?" asked Rachel.

"Four magical objects that have power over the stories we protect," said Elle. "They give the holder control of the stories. We use them to make sure that the stories go as they are supposed to, so every story ends well."

"What is Jack Frost using them for?" Kirsty asked.

"He and his goblins are using our magical objects to actually go *into* the stories and change them," said Elle. "They want the stories to be all about them."

Kirsty and Rachel exchanged a worried glance.

"So *that's* why there was a goblin in the Thumbelina story," said Rachel.

"They could spoil the stories for ever,"

said Elle,
looking
very upset.
"We have
to do
everything
we can to
stop them,
and that's why
we thought of
you. We know that
you have always been good friends of
Fairyland."

"We will help in any way we can,"
Kirsty promised. "Just tell us what you
would like us to do."

"Help me to get my magical thumb
ring back," Elle pleaded. "We'll have to
go into the story and find the goblins."

"Into the story?" Rachel repeated. "Is that possible?"

Elle gave a little smile.

"This is Fairyland," she said. "Anything is possible!"

She flicked her wand, and another book flew from the shelf and into her waiting hands. It had a pale-blue cover, and a single word was written on the front in silver letters: *Thumbelina*.

"Come a little closer," said Elle.

Rachel and Kirsty stood on either side of her, and then she waved her wand. In a cloud of rainbow-coloured glitter, the girls were swept inside the story of *Thumbelina*.

Kirsty and Rachel found themselves standing in a cottage. White lace curtains covered the tiny windows, and

there was a jug of wild flowers on the
wooden kitchen table.

"Oh, we're human again!" Rachel
exclaimed.

"Yes," said Elle. "The storybook world
is the same size as the human world.
Look."

She pointed to a little walnut shell on a nearby windowsill. It was even smaller than she was.

"This must be Thumbelina's bed," Kirsty exclaimed, hurrying over to examine it. "Yes, look, Rachel! There is a tiny pillow and a beautiful quilt made from a rose petal."

Rachel came forward too, and then paused.

"Can you hear a noise?" she asked. "It sounds like someone crying."

"Perhaps it's Thumbelina!" said Kirsty.

She flung open the window and looked down. Among the bright petals in the window box was a tiny man wearing a

golden crown. His face was buried in his hands, and he was crying as if his heart were broken.

"It must be the flower fairy prince," said Rachel in a soft voice. "He is supposed to marry Thumbelina at the end of the story."

"That's right," said Elle. "He's a cousin of the Petal Fairies."

The little prince heard them speaking and looked up. He looked horrified when he saw the girls peering down at him.

"Giants!" he cried, jumping to his feet. "Please, don't eat me!"

The Flower Prince

"Don't be scared," said Kirsty. "We're not giants – we're human girls. And we don't want to eat you – we want to help you!"

"No one can help me," groaned the prince, sinking back down into his flowery seat.

"Why?" asked Elle, flying out through the window to hover beside him. "What's happened?"

"My dearest love, Thumbelina, has been taken from me by three bright-green monsters," said the prince. "They snatched her from her walnut-shell bed and ran off with her."

"Did they have big feet?" Rachel asked.

"And long noses?" Kirsty added.

The prince nodded, and the girls exchanged knowing glances. Goblins!

"I tried to follow them," he said. "I ordered them to bring her back to me. But they just laughed and said that a tiny prince was no match for them, and they were right. There was nothing I could do to get Thumbelina away from them, so I came back here, hoping for a miracle."

"Try not to worry," Rachel said in a soothing voice. "We know exactly who those goblins are, and we've come to help. We'll rescue Thumbelina and we'll get Elle's magical thumb ring back too."

"Do you know where the goblins took Thumbelina?" Kirsty asked. "Could you take us there?"

The prince looked at the girls with a doubtful expression.

"I only know how to fly there," he said. "I'm not sure I could lead humans on foot."

"That's not a problem for us," said Elle.

She waved her wand, and in a whoosh of sparkles Rachel and Kirsty shrank to fairy size. The prince looked at them in astonishment as they fluttered towards him.

"This is marvellous!" he exclaimed.

"Come, follow me and I will lead you to where I last saw them."

He zoomed up into the sky on flower-petal wings, and the three fairies followed him. Rachel and Kirsty gazed down at the storybook world as they flew overhead. They passed over a forest and at last reached a wide, burbling stream. There was an island in the centre of the stream, and the prince stopped, hovering in midair.

"There," he said, pointing down to the island. "There they are."

Three goblins were standing around a tree stump in the middle of the island. The fairies and the prince flew closer and perched on a low-hanging tree

branch. The goblins did not notice them. They were in the middle of a loud quarrel.

"I should be the one to wear the magical thumb ring," a plump goblin was saying. "After all, I'm the one who snatched her. She should marry me!"

He was holding a silver thumb ring up, and a long-nosed goblin shoved him, knocking the ring onto the tree stump.

"Nonsense!" the long-nosed goblin said, grabbing the ring. "It fits my hand much better than yours. Besides, she smiled at me."

"I'm the oldest so she should be mine!" shrieked a knobbly-kneed goblin, snatching the ring and kissing it.

"She doesn't want to marry any of them," said the flower prince. "I am hoping that she wants to marry me! But where is she?"

They looked around, and then the prince drew in a sharp breath and grabbed Kirsty's arm.

"There she is," he said. "Look – on the tree stump."

The fairies looked and saw a tiny girl, no bigger than a human thumb, running this way and that across the tree stump. She was trying to reach out to the ring that the goblins were throwing around, but she was much too small.

"Come on, let's go and get her!" the prince exclaimed.

"Wait," said Rachel, putting her hand on his arm. "We have to get Elle's thumb ring back too, or the story won't end properly and you still won't get to marry Thumbelina."

"But we can't leave her there with those goblins!" the prince cried.

"We need to distract them," said Kirsty, thinking hard. "Could you swoop down towards them and try to keep them talking to you? Maybe we can get the thumb ring while they're not looking."

The prince nodded.

"I love Thumbelina!" he declared, throwing his tiny hands in the air. "I will do whatever it takes to rescue her!"

Brave Thumbelina

The flower prince swooped down
towards the goblins, shouting as he flew.

"Let Thumbelina go!" he demanded.
"You don't belong in our story!"

The goblins jumped up and darted
towards him, raising their hands and
trying to swat him like a fly.

"Hurray!" Thumbelina shouted, delighted to see the prince. "Now you'll be sorry!"

"No pint-sized prince is going to stop us!" the plump goblin shrieked.

Meanwhile, the three fairies zoomed down towards the goblin with the thumb ring. He wasn't paying attention to the ring – it would be easy to slip it off his thumb without him noticing. But just as Kirsty was about to grab it, the long-nosed goblin snatched it. He shoved it onto his thumb and folded his fingers over it.

"Hey, that's mine!" the knobbly-kneed goblin wailed. "Give it back!"

The goblins splashed into the shallow stream, shouting and squabbling. They pushed and shoved each other, dunking

under the water and spluttering with
fury. But all the time, the long-nosed
goblin kept dancing around in front
of them.

"I'm going to marry Thumbelina!" he
jeered in a sing-song voice. "You two
might as well go and marry toads!"

Sniggering and gloating, he danced further out into the stream, while the prince flew across to the tree stump and put his arms around Thumbelina.

"I will find a way to save you from marrying a goblin," he promised.

"But how?" asked Thumbelina with tears in her eyes. "They're so much bigger than us."

"Size doesn't matter," said Rachel, smiling at the girl. "You've got fairies and magic and friendship on your side. I know that we can stop those goblins. We just have to think of a clever plan to get the thumb ring back, and then everything will be all right."

"I don't think anything will make the goblins give up the ring," said Thumbelina. "I've been listening to them, and it's all they talk about. That, and their wedding plans for me."

"That's it!" Rachel exclaimed. "Rings are really important in weddings. We have to offer a swap. Elle, could you magic up another ring?"

Elle waved her wand, and there was a faint magical tinkle as a sparkly green ring dropped onto the tree stump beside them.

It glimmered in the sunshine, and
immediately caught the eye of the long-
nosed goblin. He splashed out of the
stream and hurried over to it, his arm
outstretched.

"Mine!" he squawked.

Kirsty seized the ring and flew
upwards, holding it out of his reach.

"If you want this, you have to return Elle's thumb ring first," she said.

"Give it!" hollered the goblin, jumping up and down and trying to reach Kirsty. "I want it now!"

Rachel fluttered up and hovered in front of the goblin.

"You're not thinking clearly," she said. "If you're going to marry Thumbelina, you have to have a ring to give her. After all, the bride and groom usually exchange rings. If Thumbelina gives you the green ring, surely you should give her the thumb ring?"

The goblin thought about this for
a moment, but he still didn't seem
convinced.

"If I were lucky enough to marry
Thumbelina, I would certainly give her
a ring," said the flower prince.

"Fine," snapped the goblin. "I'll give
Thumbelina the ring on one condition.
She has to marry me right now!"

The fairies and the flower prince
were horrified, but Thumbelina stepped
forward.

"I agree," she said.

Rachel and Kirsty stared at her in
admiration. They thought that she was
very brave.

"Thumbelina, what are you saying?"
the prince asked with a gasp.

Thumbelina smiled at him.

"Don't worry," she said quietly. "I trust you and the fairies to save me before I have to marry that horrible goblin. But the most important thing is to get the ring back. Without it, our story will never be right again."

Woodland Wedding

Thumbelina and the fairies stood on the tree stump, watching as the goblin smoothed down his bumpy head and put a moth-eaten green tie around his neck.

"Aren't you going to dress up?" he asked Thumbelina with a jeering smile. "It is your wedding day, after all."

"It isn't the wedding day I wanted," Thumbelina replied. "I'm not happy, and I don't feel like dressing up."

"I don't care," said the goblin. "I just can't wait to see the faces of the other goblins in Goblin Grotto when they see my bride!"

He rubbed his hands together and the flower prince turned away. He was worried that Thumbelina might really have to marry this horrible goblin. The other two goblins were looking very grumpy. They had found some old waistcoats for the occasion, but they were rather a tight fit.

"I will conduct the ceremony," said Elle, stepping onto the highest point of the tree stump.

Thumbelina stood in front of her, and

the goblin capered around beside the tree stump.

"First, you must exchange your rings," said Elle. "Goblin, give the bride her ring."

"Give me my ring first," said the goblin with a cunning smile.

Elle shook her head.

"The bride goes first," she said. "That's how it should be done."

Grumbling, the goblin took the thumb ring off and placed it in front of Thumbelina. It was much too big for her to wear, but she pushed it towards Elle.

As soon as the little fairy touched the ring, it shrank to its correct size. Elle slipped it onto her thumb and smiled.

"Hey, that ring's for Thumbelina!" the goblin protested. "Give it back!"

66

Kirsty handed the sparkly green ring
to Thumbelina who held it out to the
goblin.

"This is for you to keep," she said.
"But I am not going to marry you. I
will decide for myself who I'm going to
marry – and I want to marry the flower
prince."

With that,
she ran into
the prince's
arms and
the two
of them
embraced
joyfully.
Suddenly,
bells started to
chime all around them.

Rachel clapped her hands together in delight.

"They're bluebells!" she cried.

"They're telling all the woodland creatures that there will be a wedding today," said Elle.

She waved her wand, and Thumbelina's dress disappeared. In its place was a wedding gown made of white rose petals. A cobweb veil covered her face, held in place by a golden tiara.

From all around, woodland animals splashed across the stream to join them on the little island. Soon there was a huge congregation of wedding guests, and nightingales perched in the trees and sang for the happy couple.

Elle led the ceremony, and Rachel and Kirsty were bridesmaids. The prince and Thumbelina gave each other sparkling dewdrop rings.

"I now declare you husband and wife!" said Elle.

"Hurray!" cried Rachel and Kirsty. "Three cheers for Thumbelina!"

The bluebells started to chime again, and a clamour of happy noises went up from the woodland guests. Even the goblins celebrated, throwing handfuls of flower petal confetti at Thumbelina and her prince. Tears rolled down the 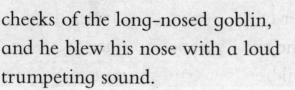 cheeks of the long-nosed goblin, and he blew his nose with a loud trumpeting sound.

"I love weddings!" he sniffed.

After the ceremony, there was dancing and a magnificent feast. Rachel and Kirsty wished that their storybook adventure could go on forever, but after a while Elle fluttered over and put her arms around them.

"It's time to go," she whispered. "Thank you for helping me to put my story right."

"Thank you for bringing us here," Kirsty replied.

Elle raised her wand, and the beautiful woodland scene disappeared in a whoosh of fairy dust. When the sparkles faded, the girls found themselves sitting beside the river at the Storytelling Festival. As usual, no time had passed since they left. The children were still sitting around the

71

book bench, and Alana Yarn was still reading *Thumbelina* aloud.

"The toad lived in a swampy stream in the garden," she said. "He croaked when he saw Thumbelina."

Rachel and Kirsty exchanged smiles of relief and happiness. The story was back to normal. They settled back to enjoy listening. When Alana came to the part about Thumbelina and the flower prince getting married, they felt a thrill of excitement.

"All their woodland friends came to the wedding, and their fairy friends, too," Alana read.

"I can't believe it!" said Rachel in a whisper. "We're in the story!"

"It was a wonderful wedding," said Kirsty. "I'll never forget it."

The best friends smiled at each other, but then Kirsty looked thoughtful.

"I wonder which story Jack Frost and the goblins will want to change next," she said. "I hope that we can get the rest of the magical objects back for the Storybook Fairies."

Rachel thought of the beautiful woodland wedding they had just seen, and the magic that Elle had performed. Then she looked around at the rapt faces of the other children.

"We will," she said, feeling determined. "Stories are too important to let Jack Frost spoil them!"

RAINBOW magic

Calling all parents, carers and teachers!
The Rainbow Magic fairies are here to help
your child enter the magical world of reading.
Whatever reading stage they are at, there's
a Rainbow Magic book for everyone!
Here is Lydia the Reading Fairy's guide to
supporting your child's journey at all levels.

Starting Out

Our Rainbow Magic Beginner Readers are perfect for first-time readers who are just beginning to develop reading skills and confidence. Approved by teachers, they contain a full range of educational levelling, as well as lively full-colour illustrations.

Developing Readers

Rainbow Magic Early Readers contain longer stories and wider vocabulary for building stamina and growing confidence. These are adaptations of our most popular Rainbow Magic stories, specially developed for younger readers in conjunction with an Early Years reading consultant, with full-colour illustrations.

Going Solo

The Rainbow Magic chapter books – a mixture of series and one-off specials – contain accessible writing to encourage your child to venture into reading independently. These highly collectible and much-loved magical stories inspire a love of reading to last a lifetime.

www.rainbowmagicbooks.co.uk

"Rainbow Magic got my daughter reading chapter books. Great sparkly covers, cute fairies and traditional stories full of magic that she found impossible to put down" – Mother of Edie (6 years)

"Florence LOVES the Rainbow Magic books. She really enjoys reading now" – Mother of Florence (6 years)

Now it's time for Kirsty and
Rachel to help...

Mariana the Goldilocks Fairy

Read on for a sneak peek...

Kirsty Tate was walking along the river
path towards the Story Barge, feeling
thrilled to her fingertips. She loved
books, and the Wetherbury Storytelling
Festival was like a dream come true for
her. Even better, she was enjoying every
moment with her best friend, Rachel
Walker, who was staying for the whole
weekend.

"This day just gets better and better,"
said Rachel, slipping her arm through
Kirsty's. "The Storybook Picnic was
truly amazing, and now we're going to
see a puppet show put on by Alana Yarn.

I can't wait!"

Alana Yarn was one of their favourite authors. She was running the festival, which was being held in Wetherbury Park. The girls were attending every event they could. They had just come from a giant picnic, where they had eaten food inspired by their favourite stories. There had even been a cake in the shape of a very large storybook.

"What was your favourite food at the picnic?" Kirsty asked as they reached the Story Barge.

"I can't decide," said Rachel after a moment's pause. "I loved the Alice in Wonderland 'Eat Me' cupcakes, but the Peter Pan fairy cakes were delicious too."

They were standing next to the Story Barge now, and there was a sign on the path advertising the show.

Alana Yarn's Puppet Show
Come along and guess the story!

"Come on!" said Kirsty.

She stepped on board the creaky old Story Barge. A short ladder led to the upper deck, which was piled with books. Inviting armchairs were dotted around, as well as plump floor cushions. Lots of children were already on board, looking very excited.

Read **Mariana the Goldilocks Fairy** to find out what adventures are in store for Kirsty and Rachel!

Meet the
Storybook Fairies

Can Rachel and Kirsty help get their new fairy friends'
magical objects back from Jack Frost, before all
their favourite stories are ruined?

www.rainbowmagicbooks.co.uk

Join in the magic online by signing up
to the Rainbow Magic fan club!

Meet the fairies, play games and
get sneak peeks at the latest books!

There's fairy fun for everyone at

www.rainbowmagicbooks.co.uk

You'll find great activities, competitions, stories and
fairy profiles, and also a special newsletter.

Find a fairy with
your name!